This book belongs to:

_____

_____

A TREASURY OF

NURSERY
RHYMES

Over 100 favourite rhymes

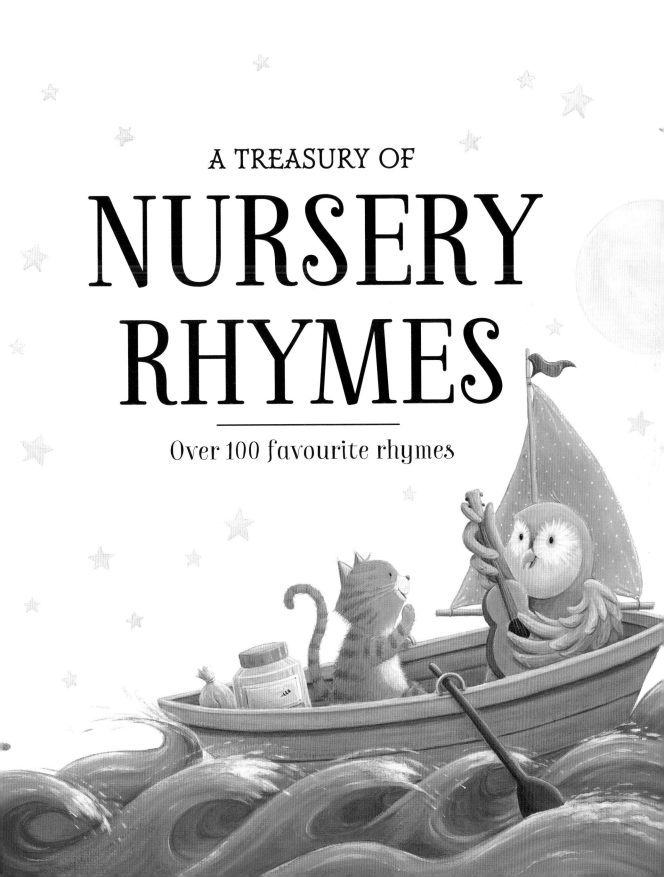

This edition published by Parragon Books Ltd in 2016

Parragon Books Ltd
Chartist House
15–17 Trim Street
Bath BA1 1HA, UK
www.parragon.com

ISBN 978-1-4748-5726-0

Printed in China

A TREASURY OF
NURSERY
RHYMES

Over 100 favourite rhymes

PaRragon

Bath • New York • Cologne • Melbourne • Delhi
Hong Kong • Shenzhen • Singapore

Contents

Classic Rhymes

Animal Rhymes

Counting Rhymes

Action Rhymes

Bedtime Rhymes

Classic Rhymes

Humpty Dumpty

Humpty Dumpty sat on a wall,
Humpty Dumpty had a

great f$_a$ll.

All the king's horses, and all the king's men
Couldn't put Humpty together again!

The Grand Old Duke Of York

The grand old Duke of York,
He had ten thousand men.
He marched them up to the top of the hill
And he marched them down again.

When they were up, they were up.
And when they were down, they were down.
And when they were only halfway up,
They were neither up nor down.

Rain, Rain, Go Away

Rain, rain, go away,
Come again another day.
Little Johnny wants to play.

One Misty, Moisty Morning

One misty, moisty morning,
When cloudy was the weather,
There I met an old man
All clothed in leather.
He began to compliment
And I began to grin.
How do you do?
And how do you do?
And how do you do
AGAIN?

Mary, Mary, Quite Contrary

Mary, Mary, quite contrary,
How does your garden grow?
With silver bells and cockle shells
And pretty maids all in a row.

Old King Cole

Old King Cole was a merry old soul
And a merry old soul was he.
He called for his pipe in the middle of the night
And he called for his fiddlers three.

Every fiddler had a very fine fiddle
And a very fine fiddle had he.
Oh there's none so rare as can compare,
With King Cole and his fiddlers three.

Hector Protector

Hector Protector was dressed all in green,
Hector Protector was sent to the queen.
The queen did not like him,
No more did the king,
So Hector Protector was sent back again.

See-Saw, Margery Daw

See-saw, Margery Daw,
Johnny shall have a new master.
He shall have but a penny a day,
Because he can't work any faster.

There Was An Old Woman

There was an old woman
Who lived in a shoe.
She had so many children
She didn't know what to do!

So she gave them some broth
Without any bread.
Then she whipped them all soundly
And sent them to bed.

23

What Are Little Boys Made Of?

What are little boys made of?
What are little boys made of?
Snips and snails,
And puppy-dogs' tails,
That's what little boys are made of.

What Are Little Girls Made Of?

What are little girls made of?
What are little girls made of?

Sugar and spice,
And all things nice,

That's what little girls are made of.

A Sailor Went To Sea

A sailor went to sea, sea, sea.
To see what he could see, see, see.
But all that he could see, see, see,

Was
the
bottom
of the
deep
blue
sea,
sea, sea.

Long-Legged Sailor

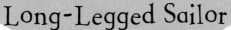

Have you ever, ever, ever,
in your long-legged life
met a long-legged sailor
with a long-legged wife?

No, I never, never, never,
in my long-legged life
met a long-legged sailor
with a long-legged wife.

*(Repeat the rhyme four more times,
using the different words.)*

Have you ever, ever, ever,
in your short-legged life...

Have you ever, ever, ever,
in your knock-kneed life...

Have you ever, ever, ever,
in your pigeon-toed life...

Have you ever, ever, ever,
in your bow-legged life...

Monday's Child

Monday's child is fair of face,
Tuesday's child is full of grace,
Wednesday's child is full of woe,
Thursday's child has far to go,

Friday's child is loving and giving,
Saturday's child works hard for his living,
And the child that is born on the Sabbath day
Is bonny and blithe and good and gay.

There Was A Little Girl

There was a little girl
And she had a little curl,
Right in the middle
Of her forehead.

When she was good,
She was very, very good.
But when she was bad,
She was...

Horrid.

Little Tommy Tucker

Little Tommy Tucker sings for his supper.
What shall we give him? Brown bread and butter.
How shall he cut it without a knife?
How shall he marry without a wife?

Lavender's Blue

Lavender's blue, dilly, dilly,
Lavender's green,
When I am king, dilly, dilly,
You shall be queen.

Call up your men, dilly, dilly,
Set them to work,
Some with a rake, dilly, dilly,
Some with a fork.

Some to make hay, dilly, dilly,
Some to thresh corn,
While you and I, dilly, dilly,
Keep ourselves warm.

The Queen Of Hearts

The Queen of Hearts, she made some tarts
All on a summer's day.
The Knave of Hearts, he stole the tarts
And took them clean away.

The King of Hearts called for the tarts
And beat the Knave full sore.
The Knave of Hearts brought back the tarts
And vowed he'd steal no more.

The Big Ship Sails

The big ship sails on the ally-ally-oh,
The ally-ally-oh, the ally-ally-oh.
Oh, the big ship sails on the ally-ally-oh
On the last day of September.

The captain said it will never, never do,
Never, never do, never, never do.
The captain said it will never, never do
On the last day of September.

The big ship sank to the bottom of the sea,
The bottom of the sea, the bottom of the sea.
The big ship sank to the bottom of the sea
On the last day of September.

We all dip our heads in the deep blue sea,
The deep blue sea, the deep blue sea.
We all dip our heads in the deep blue sea
On the last day of September.

Oats And Beans And Barley Grow

Oats and beans and barley grow,
Oats and beans and barley grow.
Do you or I or anyone know
How oats and beans and barley grow?

First the farmer sows his seed,
Then he stands and takes his ease.
Stamps his feet and claps his hands
And turns around to view his lands.

Oats and beans and barley grow,
Oats and beans and barley grow.
Do you or I or anyone know
How oats and beans and barley grow?

There Was A Crooked Man

There was a crooked man
And he walked a crooked mile,
He found a crooked sixpence
Upon a crooked stile.

40

He bought a crooked cat,
Which caught a crooked mouse,
And they all lived together
In a little crooked house.

Hickory Dickory Dock

Hickory dickory dock,
The mouse ran up the clock.
The clock struck one,
The mouse ran down,
Hickory dickory dock.

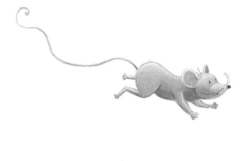

Tweedledum And Tweedledee

Tweedledum and Tweedledee
Agreed to have a battle,
For Tweedledum said Tweedledee
Had spoiled his nice new rattle.

Just then flew down a monstrous crow,
As black as a tar-barrel,
Which frightened both the heroes so,
They quite forgot their quarrel.

43

Little Miss Muffet

Little Miss Muffet
Sat on a tuffet,
Eating her curds and whey.

Along came a spider,
Who sat down beside her

And frightened Miss Muffet away!

Betty Botter Bought Some Butter

Betty Botter bought some butter,
But she said, "The butter's bitter.
If I put it in my batter,
It will make my batter bitter.
But a bit of better butter
Will make my batter better."

So she bought some better butter.
Better than the bitter butter,
And she put it in her batter.
And her batter was not bitter.
So 'twas better Betty Botter
Bought a bit of better butter.

Animal Rhymes

Little Bo-Peep

Little Bo-Peep has lost her sheep
And doesn't know where to find them.

48

Leave them alone
And they'll come home,
Wagging their tails behind them.

Baa, Baa, Black Sheep

Baa, baa, black sheep,
Have you any wool?

Yes sir, yes sir,
Three bags full.

One for the master...

And one for the dame...

And one for the little boy
Who lives down the lane.

Once I Saw A Little Bird

Once I saw a little bird
Come hop, hop, hop.
So I cried, "Little bird,
Will you STOP, STOP, STOP?"
I was going to the window,
To say, "How do you do?"
But he shook his little tail,
And far away he flew.

Hickety Pickety

Hickety Pickety, my black hen,
She lays eggs for gentlemen,
Sometimes nine, and sometimes ten,
Hickety Pickety, my black hen!

Hey Diddle Diddle

Hey diddle diddle, the cat and the fiddle,

The cow jumped over the moon.

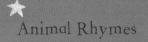

The little dog laughed to see such fun

And the dish ran away with the spoon!

The Owl And The Pussy Cat

The Owl and the Pussy Cat went to sea
In a beautiful pea-green boat,
They took some honey, and plenty of money,
Wrapped up in a five pound note.

The Owl looked up to the stars above,
And sang to a small guitar,
"Oh lovely Pussy! Oh Pussy, my love,
What a beautiful Pussy you are, you are, you are,
What a beautiful Pussy you are."

Pussy said to the Owl, "You elegant fowl,
How charmingly sweet you sing.
Oh let us be married, too long we have tarried.
But what shall we do for a ring?"

They sailed away, for a year and a day,
To the land where the Bong-tree grows,
And there in a wood a Piggy-wig stood
With a ring at the end of his nose, his nose, his nose,
With a ring at the end of his nose.

Old Mother Hubbard

Old Mother Hubbard
Went to the cupboard,
To get her poor doggie a bone.
But when she got there
The cupboard was bare,
So her poor little doggie had none.

Higglety, Pigglety, Pop!

The dog has eaten the mop,

The pig's in a hurry,

The cat's in a flurry,

Higglety, pigglety, POP!

Three Young Rats

Three young rats with black felt hats,
Three young ducks with white straw flats,

Three young dogs with curling tails,
Three young cats with demi-veils,

Went out to walk with two young pigs
In satin vests and sorrel wigs.

But suddenly it chanced to rain
And so they all went home again.

I Had A Little Puppy

I had a little puppy
His name was Tiny Tim.

I put him in the bathtub,
To see if he could swim.

He drank all the water,
He ate a bar of soap.
The next thing you know
He had a bubble in his throat.

Mary Had A Little Lamb

Mary had a little lamb,
Its fleece was white as snow,
And everywhere that Mary went

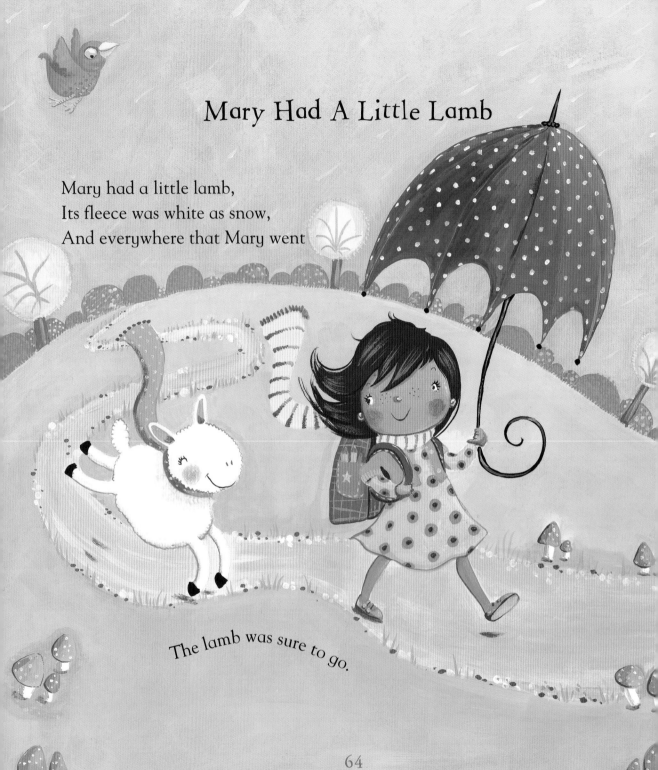

The lamb was sure to go.

It followed her to school one day,
Which was against the rule.
It made the children laugh and play
To see a lamb at school.

Miss Mary Mack

Miss Mary Mack,
All dressed in black,
With silver buttons,
All down her back,
She asked her mother,
For fifty cents,

To see the elephant,
Jump the fence,
He jumped so high,
He touched the sky,
And didn't come back,
Till the Fourth of July.

The Lion And The Unicorn

The lion and the unicorn were fighting for the crown.
The lion beat the unicorn all around the town.
Some gave them white bread,
And some gave them brown,
Some gave them plum cake,
And drummed them out of town.

Horsie, Horsie

Horsie, horsie, don't you stop,
Just let your feet go clippety clop,
Your tail goes swish,
And the wheels go round,

Giddy-up, you're homeward bound!

I Had A Little Hobby Horse

I had a little hobby horse,
And it was dapple grey.
Its head was made of pea-straw,
Its tail was made of hay.

I sold it to an old woman
For a copper groat,
And I'll not sing my song again
Without another coat.

I Had A Little Hen

I had a little hen,
The prettiest ever seen,
She washed up the dishes,
And kept the house clean.

She went to the mill
To fetch me some flour,
And always got home
In less than an hour.

She baked me my bread,
She brewed me my ale,
She sat by the fire
And told a fine tale!

71

Sing A Song Of Sixpence

Sing a song of sixpence
A pocket full of rye.
Four and twenty blackbirds
Baked in a pie.
When the pie was opened
The birds began to sing.
Now wasn't that a dainty dish
To set before the king?

The king was in his counting house
Counting out his money.
The queen was in the parlour
Eating bread and honey.
The maid was in the garden
Hanging out the clothes,
When down came a blackbird
And pecked off
her nose!

Pussy Cat, Pussy Cat

Pussy cat, pussy cat,
Where have you been?
I've been to London
To visit the Queen.
Pussy cat, pussy cat,
What did you there?
I frightened a little mouse
Under her chair.

Three Blind Mice

Three blind mice, three blind mice,
See how they run, see how they run!
They all ran after the farmer's wife,
Who cut off their tails with a carving knife,
Did you ever see such a thing in your life
As three blind mice?

Ding Dong Bell

Ding dong bell,
Pussy's in the well.
Who put her in?
Little Johnny Flynn.
Who pulled her out?
Little Tommy Stout.
What a naughty boy was that
To try to drown poor Pussy Cat,
Who never did any harm
But killed all the mice
In the farmer's barn!

Counting
Rhymes

Two Little Dickie Birds

Two little dickie birds sitting on a wall,
One named Peter, one named Paul.

Fly away Peter, fly away Paul.

Come back Peter, come back Paul.

One Potato, Two Potato

One potato,

Two potato,

Three potato,

Four.

Five potato,

Six potato,

Seven potato,

More!

Five Little Ducks

Five little ducks went swimming one day,
Over the hills and far away.
Mother Duck said, "Quack, quack, quack, quack,"
But only four little ducks came back.

*(Repeat the rhyme, counting down from four little ducks
to one little duck…)*

One little duck went swimming one day,
Over the hills and far away.
Mother Duck said, "Quack, quack, quack, quack,"
But none of the five little ducks came back.

Mother Duck went swimming one day,
Over the hills and far away.
Mother Duck said, "Quack, quack, quack, quack,"
And five little ducks came swimming back.

Eeny, Meeny

Eeny, meeny, miney, mo,
Catch a tiger by the toe,

If he squeals let him go,
Eeny, meeny, miney, mo.

85

Five Fat Peas

Five fat peas in a pea-pod pressed,
One grew, two grew, so did all the rest.

They grew, and grew,
And did not stop,
Until one day,

the pod went
POP!

One Man Went To Mow

One man went to mow,
Went to mow a meadow,
One man, and his dog,
Went to mow a meadow.

Two men went to mow,
Went to mow a meadow,
Two men, one man, and his dog,
Went to mow a meadow.

Three men went to mow,
Went to mow a meadow,
Three men, two men,
one man, and his dog,
Went to mow a meadow.

Four men went to mow,
Went to mow a meadow,
Four men, three men, two men,
one man, and his dog,
Went to mow a meadow.
*(You can keep adding verses as far
as you can count.)*

One, Two, Buckle My Shoe

One, two, buckle my shoe,

Three, four, knock at the door,

Five, six, pick up sticks,

Seven, eight, lay them straight,

Nine, ten, a big fat hen,

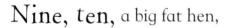

Eleven, twelve,
dig and delve,

Thirteen, fourteen,
maids a-courting,

Fifteen, sixteen,
maids in the kitchen,

Seventeen, eighteen,
maids in waiting,

Nineteen, twenty,
my plate's empty!

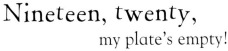

One, Two, Three, Four, Five

One, two, three, four, five,
Once I caught a fish alive.
Six, seven, eight, nine, ten,
Then I let it go again.

Why did you let it go?
Because it bit my finger so.
Which finger did it bite?
This little finger on the right.

Five Little Monkeys

Five little monkeys jumping on the bed,
One fell off and bumped his head.
Mama called the Doctor and the Doctor said,
"No more monkeys jumping on the bed!"

Four little monkeys jumping on the bed,
One fell off and bumped her head.
Papa called the Doctor and the Doctor said,
"No more monkeys jumping on the bed!"

*(Repeat the rhyme, counting down from three
little monkeys to one little monkey…)*

One little monkey jumping on the bed,
He fell off and bumped his head.
Mama called the Doctor and the Doctor said,
"Put those monkeys straight to bed!"

One For Sorrow

One for sorrow,

Two for joy,

Three for a girl,

Four for a boy,

Five for silver,

Six for gold,

Seven for a secret, never to be told.

This Old Man

This old man, he played one,
He played knick-knack on my drum.

(Chorus)

With a knick-knack, paddy whack,
Give a dog a bone,
This old man came rolling home.

This old man, he played two,
He played knick-knack on my shoe.

(Chorus)

This old man, he played three,
He played knick-knack on my knee.

(Chorus)

This old man, he played four,
He played knick-knack on my door.

(Chorus)

This old man, he played five,
He played knick-knack on my hive.

(*Chorus*)

This old man, he played six,
He played knick-knack on my sticks.

(*Chorus*)

This old man, he played seven,
He played knick-knack up to heaven.

(*Chorus*)

This old man, he played eight,
He played knick-knack on my gate.

(*Chorus*)

This old man, he played nine,
He played knick-knack on my spine.

(*Chorus*)

This old man, he played ten,
He played knick-knack once again.

(*Chorus*)

Ten Green Bottles

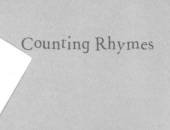

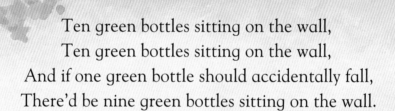

Ten green bottles sitting on the wall,
Ten green bottles sitting on the wall,
And if one green bottle should accidentally fall,
There'd be nine green bottles sitting on the wall.

Nine green bottles sitting on the wall,
Nine green bottles sitting on the wall,
And if one green bottle should accidentally fall,
There'd be eight green bottles sitting on the wall.

Eight green bottles sitting on the wall,
Eight green bottles sitting on the wall,
And if one green bottle should accidentally fall,
There'd be seven green bottles sitting on the wall.

Seven green bottles sitting on the wall,
Seven green bottles sitting on the wall,
And if one green bottle should accidentally fall,
There'd be six green bottles sitting on the wall.

(You can keep adding verses until there are no more bottles!)

Rub-A-Dub-Dub

Rub-a-dub-dub,
Three men in a tub,
And how do you think they got there?

The butcher, the baker
The candlestick maker,

They all jumped out of a rotten potato,
It was enough to make a man stare.

Five Fat Sausages

Five fat sausages sizzling in the pan,
All of a sudden one went

BANG!

Four fat sausages sizzling in the pan,
All of a sudden one went

BANG!

Three fat sausages sizzling in the pan,
All of a sudden one went

BANG!

Two fat sausages sizzling in the pan,
All of a sudden one went

BANG!

One fat sausage sizzling in the pan,
All of a sudden it went

BANG!

Each Peach, Pear, Plum

Each peach,

pear,

plum,

Out goes Tom Thumb.
Tom Thumb won't do,
Out goes Betty Blue.
Betty Blue won't go,
So out goes you.

Five Currant Buns

Five currant buns in the baker's shop,
Big and round with a cherry on the top.
Along came *(insert name)* with a penny one day,
Bought a currant bun and took it away.

Four currant buns in the baker's shop,
Big and round with a cherry on the top.
Along came *(insert name)* with a penny one day,
Bought a currant bun and took it away.

*(Repeat the rhyme, counting down from
three currant buns to no currant buns...)*

No currant buns in the baker's shop,
Nothing big and round with a cherry on the top.
Along came (*insert name*) with a penny one day,
"Sorry," said the baker,
"No more currant buns today."

Five Little Speckled Frogs

Five little speckled frogs,
Sat on a speckled log,
Eating the most delicious bugs,
Yum, yum!
One jumped into the pool,
Where it was nice and cool.
Now there are four green speckled frogs,
Glub, glub!

(Repeat the rhyme, counting down from five little
speckled frogs to one little speckled frog…)

One little speckled frog,
Sat on a speckled log,
Eating the most delicious bugs,
Yum, yum!
He jumped into the pool,
Where it was nice and cool.
Now there are no green speckled frogs,

Glub, glub!

Hot Cross Buns!

Hot cross buns!
Hot cross buns!
One a penny, two a penny,
Hot cross buns!
If you have no daughters,
Give them to your sons.
One a penny, two a penny,
Hot cross buns!

Action Rhymes

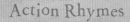

Row, Row, Row Your Boat

(Mime a rowing action throughout as the rhyme suggests.)

Row, row, row your boat
Gently down the stream.
Merrily, merrily,
merrily, merrily,

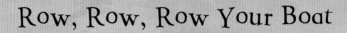

Life is but a dream.

117

I'm A Little Teapot

I'm a little teapot, short and stout,

Here's my handle,

(Place one hand on your hip.)

118

here's my spout.

(Other arm out with elbow and wrist bent.)

When I get my steam up hear me shout,

Tip me up and
pour me out.

(Lean over as if you're pouring out the tea.)

Catch It If You Can

Mix a pancake,
Beat a pancake,
Put it in a pan.
Cook a pancake,
Toss a pancake,
Catch it if you can!

Georgie Porgie

Georgie Porgie, pudding and pie,
Kissed the girls, and made them cry.
When the boys came out to play,
Georgie Porgie ran away.

Round And Round The Garden

Round and round the garden
Like a teddy bear.
*(Draw a circle on the palm of your baby's hand
with your finger.)*

Action Rhymes

One step,
Two steps,
(Walk your fingers up your baby's arm.)

Tickle you under there!
(Tickle baby under the arm.)

123

This Little Piggy

(Pretend each of the child's toes is a little piggy.
Begin with the biggest toe and finish by tickling under the child's foot.)

This little piggy
went to market,

This little piggy
stayed at home,

This little piggy
had roast beef,

This little piggy
had none,

And this little piggy cried,
"Wee, wee, wee!"
all the way home.

I Hear Thunder

I hear thunder, I hear thunder,
Hark, don't you? Hark, don't you?
Pitter-patter raindrops,
Pitter-patter raindrops,

I'm wet through,
So are you.

Pat-A-Cake, Pat-A-Cake

Pat-a-cake, pat-a-cake, baker's man,
Bake me a cake as fast as you can.
(Clap in rhythm.)

Pat it and prick it and mark it with B,
*(Pat and 'prick' palm,
then trace the letter B on palm.)*

And put it in the oven for Baby and me!
(Action of putting cake in oven.)

Incy Wincy Spider

Incy Wincy Spider
Climbing up the spout.
Down came the rain
And washed the spider out.

Out came the sun
And dried up all the rain.
Incy Wincy Spider
Climbed up the spout again.

The Wheels On The Bus

The wheels on the bus go
Round and round!

Round and round!
Round and round!

The wheels on the bus go

round...

and...**round!** **All day long.**

(Move hands in a circular motion.)

The wipers on the bus go
Swish, swish, swish!

Swish, swish, swish!
Swish, swish, swish!

The wipers on the bus go
Swish, swish, swish!

All day long.

(Wiggle both index fingers.)

The horn on the bus goes
  Beep, beep, beep!

Beep, beep, beep!
Beep, beep, beep!

The horn on the bus goes
  Beep, beep, beep!

The people on the bus go
  Chat, chat, chat!

Chat, chat, chat!
Chat, chat, chat!

The people on the bus go
  Chat, chat, chat!

All day long.

(Pretend to press a horn.)

All day long.

*(Hold your thumb and fingers out straight
to make a beak shape and open and close it.)*

Here Is The Church

Here is the church,
(Interlace fingers.)

Here is the steeple,
*(Put up both pointing fingers
to make a steeple.)*

Look inside…
(Turn both hands over.)

And see all the people!
(Wiggle your fingers.)

135

This Is The way

This is the way we wash our hands,
Wash our hands, wash our hands.
This is the way we wash our hands
So early in the morning.

*(Repeat the rhyme four more times,
using these different actions.)*

This is the way we wash our face.

This is the way we
brush our teeth.

This is the way we
comb our hair.

This is the way
we wave goodbye.

Ten In The Bed

There were ten in the bed and the little one said,
"Roll over, roll over."
So they all rolled over and one fell out.

There were nine in the bed and the little one said,
"Roll over, roll over."
So they all rolled over and one fell out.

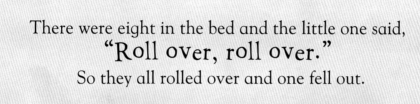

There were eight in the bed and the little one said,
"Roll over, roll over."
So they all rolled over and one fell out.

There were seven in the bed and the little one said,
"Roll over, roll over."
So they all rolled over and one fell out.

There were six in the bed and the little one said,
"Roll over, roll over."
So they all rolled over and one fell out.

(Repeat the rhyme, counting down from five in the bed
to one in the bed…)

There was one in the bed and the little one said,
"Goodnight!"

Here We Go Round The Mulberry Bush

Here we go round the mulberry bush,
The mulberry bush, the mulberry bush.
Here we go round the mulberry bush,
On a cold and frosty morning.

(Repeat the
rhyme three more times,
using these different actions.)

This is the way we
clean the house.

This is the way we
wash our clothes.

This is the way we
sweep the floor.

Ring-A-Ring O' Roses

Ring-a-ring o' roses,
A pocket full of posies.

A-tishoo! A-tishoo!
We all fall down.

Ride A Cock-Horse

Ride a cock-horse to Banbury Cross
To see a fine lady upon a white horse.
With rings on her fingers and bells on her toes,
She shall have music wherever she goes.

146

147

Sippity Sup, Sippity Sup

Sippity sup, sippity sup,
Bread and milk from a china cup.
Bread and milk from a bright silver spoon
Made of a piece of the bright silver moon.

Sippity sup, sippity sup,
Sippity,
sippity sup.

148

Bedtime Rhymes

Come To Bed, Says Sleepy-Head

"Come to bed," says Sleepy-head,

"Tarry a while," says Slow,

"Put on the pot," says Greedy-guts,

"Let's sup before we go."

Boys And Girls

Boys and girls, come out to play,
The moon doth shine as bright as day!
Leave your supper and leave your sleep,

And meet your playfellows in the street.
Come with a whoop and come with a call,
Come with a good will or not at all.

Bed In Summer

In winter I get up at night,
And dress by yellow candle-light.
In summer, quite the other way,
I have to go to bed by day.

I have to go to bed and see
The birds still hopping on the tree,
Or hear the grown-up people's feet
Still going past me in the street.

And does it not seem hard to you,
When all the sky is clear and blue,
And I should like so much to play,
To have to go to bed by day?

Brahms' Lullaby

Lullaby, and good night,
With rosy bed light,
With lilies overspread,
Is my baby's sweet bed.

Lay you down now, and rest,
May your slumber be blessed!
Lay you down now, and rest,
May your slumber be blessed!

Lullaby, and good night,
You're your mother's delight,
Shining angels beside
My darling abide.

Soft and warm is your bed,
Close your eyes and rest your head.
Soft and warm is your bed,
Close your eyes and rest your head.

Twinkle, Twinkle, Little Star

Twinkle, twinkle, little star,
How I wonder what you are!
Up above the world so high,
Like a diamond in the sky.

When the blazing sun is gone,
When he nothing shines upon,
Then you show your little light,
Twinkle, twinkle all the night.

Then the traveller in the dark,
Thanks you for your tiny spark,
He could not see which way to go,
If you did not twinkle so.

In the dark blue sky you keep,
And often through my curtains peep,
For you never shut your eye,
Till the sun is in the sky.

As your bright and tiny spark,
Lights the traveller in the dark.
Though I know not what you are,

Twinkle, twinkle, little star.

Go To Bed Late

Go to bed late,
Stay very small.

Go to bed early,
Grow very tall.

Go To Bed, Tom

Go to bed, Tom,
Go to bed, Tom,
Tired or not, Tom,
Go to bed, Tom.

Now The Day Is Over

Now the day is over,
Night is drawing nigh,
Shadows of the evening
Steal across the sky.

Now the darkness gathers,
Stars begins to peep,
Birds and beasts and flowers
Soon will be asleep.

163

Golden Slumbers

Golden slumbers kiss your eyes,
Smiles await you when you rise.
Sleep, pretty baby, do not cry,

And I will sing
a lullaby.

165

Wee Willie Winkie

Wee Willie Winkie
Runs through the town,
Upstairs and downstairs
In his nightgown.

Rapping at the window,
Crying through the lock,
"Are the children all in bed?
It's past eight o'clock."

How Many Miles To Babylon?

How many miles to Babylon?
Three score and ten.
Can I get there by candle-light?
Yes, and back again.

BABYLON

If your heels are nimble and light,
You may get there by candle-light.

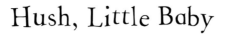

Hush, Little Baby

Hush, little baby, don't say a word,
Papa's gonna buy you a mocking bird.

If that mocking bird don't sing,
Papa's gonna buy you a diamond ring.

If that diamond ring turns to brass,
Papa's gonna buy you a looking-glass.

If that looking-glass gets broke,
Papa's gonna buy you a billy goat.

If that billy goat don't pull,
Papa's gonna buy you a cart and mule.

If that cart and mule turn over,
Papa's gonna buy you a dog named Rover.

If that dog named Rover won't bark,
Papa's gonna buy you a horse and cart.

If that horse and cart fall down,
You'll still be the sweetest little baby in town.

Rock-A-Bye, Baby

Rock-a-bye, baby, on the tree top,
When the wind blows, the cradle will rock.

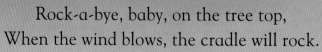

When the bough breaks,
The cradle will fall,

Down will come baby, cradle and all.

Jack Be Nimble

Jack be nimble,
Jack be quick,

Jack jump over…

the candlestick.

Jack And Jill

Jack and Jill went up the hill
To fetch a pail of water,
Jack fell down and broke his crown,

And Jill came tumbling after.

Up Jack got, and home did trot
As fast as he could caper,
He went to bed, to mend his head,
With vinegar and brown paper.

Sleep, Little Child

Sleep, little child, go to sleep,
Mother is here by your bed.
Sleep, little child, go to sleep,
Rest on the pillow your head.

Bedtime Rhymes

The world is silent and still,
The moon shines bright on the hill,
Then creeps past the window sill.
Oh sleep, go to sleep.

Diddle, Diddle, Dumpling

Diddle, diddle, dumpling, my son John,
  Went to bed with his trousers on,

One shoe off,

and the other shoe on,

Diddle, diddle, dumpling, my son John.

It's Raining, It's Pouring

It's raining, it's pouring,
The old man is snoring.

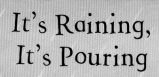

He went to bed and he bumped his head,
And couldn't get up in the morning.

Little Fred

When little Fred went to bed,
He always said his prayers,
He kissed Mum, and then Papa,

And straightaway went upstairs.

185

Go To Bed First

Go to bed first,
A golden purse,

Go to bed second,
A golden pheasant,

Go to bed third,
A golden bird.

Star Light, Star Bright

Star light,
Star bright,
First star
I see tonight,

I wish I may,
I wish I might,
Have the wish
I wish tonight.

Index Of First Lines